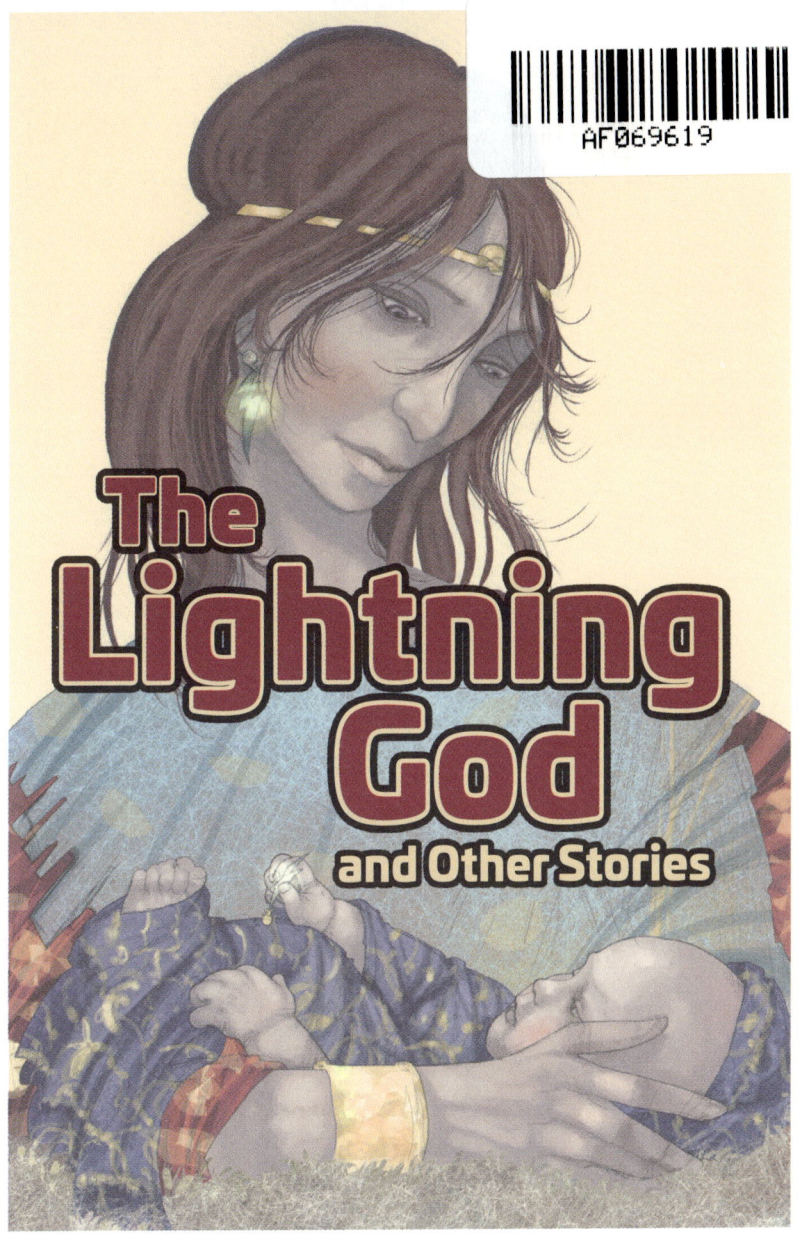

The Lightning God
and Other Stories

Collins

Contents

Unit 1: Refer to Code planning.

Core

Unit 2: Hidden Amazon 6

Unit 3: Fantastic Greek Facts 13

Unit 4: Travelling Animals 20

Unit 5: The Thrill Factor 27

Challenge

Unit 2: The Alhambra 36

Unit 3: The Lightning God 43

Unit 4: Shark Attack 50

Unit 5: Storm! 57

Consolidate

Unit 2: Travel to TRAPPIST-1e 66

Unit 3: Lightwing 73

Unit 4: Killer Instinct 80

Unit 5: Dragon Quest 87

Core texts

Hidden Amazon

| ai | ee |

| many | whole | don't | made | one | very | move |

Hidden Amazon is a non-fiction text that looks at some unusual inhabitants of the Amazon rainforest. It's hard to see beyond the incredible animals and magnificent trees of the Amazon. But if you stop and look down, you might see something extraordinary. The ants of the Amazon not only make up a third of its animal **mass**, but they also tend to trees, garden **fungus** and **patrol** forest **trails**, attacking any animals that might harm the plants that they protect! The Amazon is a complex **habitat**. Read on to find out what we are learning about some of its lesser-known plants and animals.

Vocabulary:
- **mass:** the amount of something
- **fungus:** mushrooms
- **patrol:** keep watch on an area by travelling around it
- **trails:** paths
- **habitat:** a natural environment where plants or animals live or grow

How would you feel about finding a 45 cm-long leech?

Hidden Amazon

From mega moths to laidback sloths, the Amazon rainforest in Brazil has it all!

Many people travel to the Amazon to see the stunning trees and incredible animals.

But what connects the biggest trees to the littlest insects?

Trees need ants

Ants have talents that benefit the whole rainforest. Deep in the rainforest, lemon ants nest in trees. They protect hundreds of trees, killing seedlings and saplings that the ants don't need. Ant patrols sweep the forest trails to keep insects and animals from attacking their trees.

> **Fact!**
> 30% of the animal mass in the Amazon is made up of ANTS.

Lemon ants nest in stems.

Some ants help feed trees. They collect bits of plants. Fungus feeds on the plants and makes them into rich mulch. This mulch benefits the whole forest habitat.

Fungus helps ants make mulch.

Seeking leeches!

This is one of the biggest leeches in the Amazon.

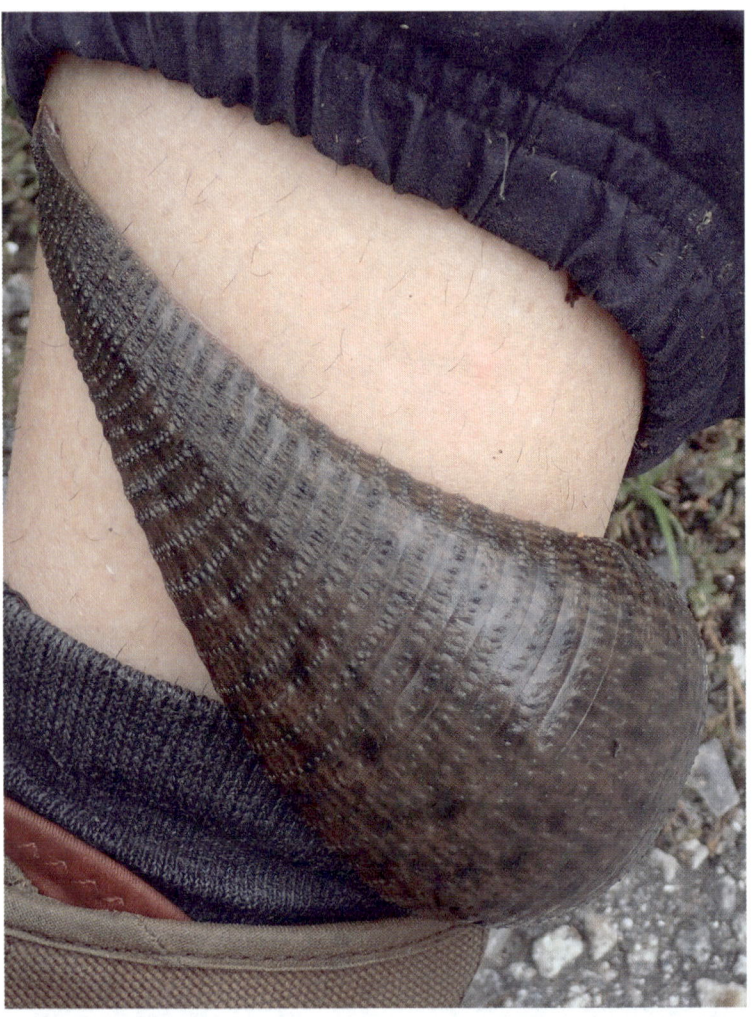

It gets up to 45 cm long!

These leeches don't need to feed very often. They wait in the mud until they feel an animal move in the water. Then the leech stabs the animal's skin and sucks as the animal bleeds! Adult leeches can feed on anacondas, caimans and cattle!

But don't be afraid. These leeches help us respond to many medical problems.

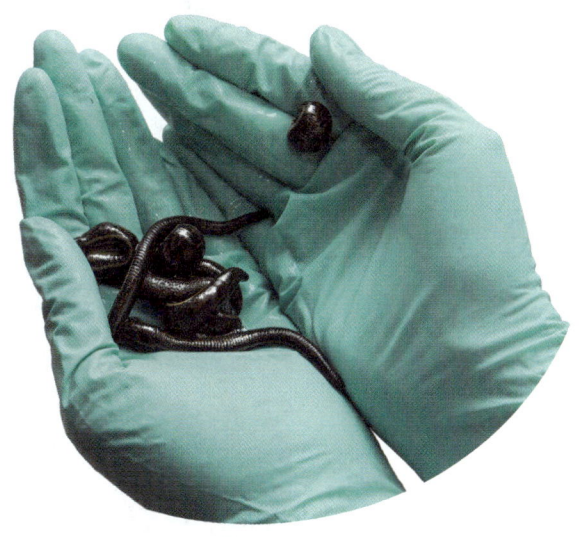

Two trees?

A fig tree begins as a little plant on a big tree.

Its green tendrils creep along the trunk, seeking the sun. In the end, the fig strangles and kills the tree. The rotten tree attracts fungus and insects. And the fig tree becomes a habitat, feeding hundreds of insects and animals.

Fantastic Greek Facts

| igh | oa |

| many | today | houses | time | thought |

Fantastic Greek Facts is a non-fiction text that uncovers some surprising things you might not know about Ancient Greece.

Ancient Greece was a civilisation in the Mediterranean that existed over 2500 years ago. It lasted for a long time: over a thousand years. You might be surprised to hear of some of the everyday objects that were **invented** by the Greeks. And you might also be a bit shocked about how much they enjoyed **combat**. They even created a sport called Pankration that involved kicking, boxing, wrestling and some cheating. It was held in a special pit called a **skamma**! **Contestants** were **coached** on how to fight, and **tactics** were mainly to be quick!

Vocabulary:
- **invented:** made something that did not exist before
- **combat:** fighting
- **skamma:** an area of a stadium, often a pit, used for Pankration matches
- **contestants:** people taking part (e.g. in a sport)
- **coached:** taught how to improve in a sport or skill
- **tactics:** a plan of how to win

What do you think the Ancient Greeks invented that we still use today?

FANTASTIC GREEK FACTS

The Greeks lived back in 800 BCE to 600 CE, but they made a big impact. The Greeks can boast that they invented many things that we still have today.

Here are some highlights of what the Greeks invented:

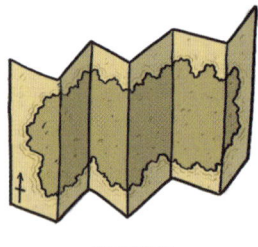

maps

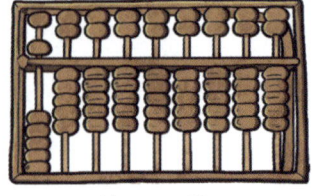

mathematics

lighthouses

bathtubs

Quick facts

Do you have a clock that beeps? Well, the Greeks invented that! But their clock didn't beep – it dropped rocks onto a gong. That might get you out of bed!

They invented a very quick sailboat. They sailed it into combat, roaming from coast to coast.

When they had a pain, the Greeks had a frightening trick to help. They put an electric fish onto the spot that hurt, to fight the pain. Shocking!

Spotlight on: Athletics

The Greeks invented athletics events to test fitness. Men were coached in fighting and combat skills.

The Greeks loved chucking loads of objects, like the javelin, discus and shot put.

And the long jump? That's right – the Greeks invented it! But in Greek times, they held a big rock when they jumped. What a sight!

The Greeks invented a combat event that mixed boxing and kicking. People flocked to the 'skamma' to see the fights. The best approach to win was with speed, but contestants needed tactics as well.

Spotlight on: Gods

As well as inventing things, the Greeks spent a lot of time respecting their gods.

They thought the gods lived high up on a hill next to Athens.

There were gods and goddesses of loads of things, like wisdom, light and luck.

The Greeks thought they would be punished if the gods were upset. Disrespect the gods and you might spend the rest of time pushing a rock up a hill!

Travelling Animals

| er | ar |

| their | very | move | we're | people |

Travelling Animals is a series of poems about animals from all over the world.

Animals travel across the globe for many reasons: to find food, to migrate, and even to find a mate. Each poem introduces a new animal. Meet the basking shark – a **drifter** of the seas, with its huge **cavern**-like mouth feeding on **unsuspecting** plankton. And the albatross, that flies along **wind-swept coasts** seeking its partner. Fish travel, too! Find out what mackerel feel about the waters they swim in, and how the allis shad swims up rivers to lay its eggs. Or how about the nightjar, a bird that travels to the UK each spring from southern Africa to camouflage itself as tree bark on our forest floors.

Vocabulary:
- **drifter:** something that is always moving
- **cavern:** a large, dark space, like a cave
- **unsuspecting:** not aware (e.g. of danger)
- **wind-swept:** where strong winds have blown the trees and plants about
- **coasts:** places where the land meets the sea

Which of these animals do you think makes the longest journey?

Travelling Animals

Arctic tern

From the summer in Antarctica
To the summer in the Arctic,
Off they go,
Arctic terns.

Criss-crossing the planet,
Seeking sunlight,
Darting at speed
From winter's chill.

High, so high
They sleep in flight.
Arctic terns.
Floating
To the freedom
Of endless summer.

Basking shark

Some sharks are hunters,
Lobster crushers,
Squid guzzlers,
Mackerel munchers.

Not basking sharks.

They are tender drifters,
Filter-feeders, floating
Like living caverns,
Gulping unsuspecting plankton
In their deep, dark traps.

Basking sharks.

Plankton grabbers,
Float from the coasts
Of Scotland to Brazil.
Chilled-out mega chompers.

Albatross

The albatross has wings
Like long unfolding maps,
High in flight
Off the wind-swept coasts
Of Antarctica.

But this albatross is very lost.

Far from Antarctica,
he seeks his long-lost partner

in England.

He never stops thinking of her,
But it is harder than ever to remember.

Albatross clings on, keeps faith,
But it is hard, so hard.

And he is lost.

Mackerel

"I like it hot," said Mackerel,
"But when it's cold it's better."

"We mackerel move in patterns,
Like starlings, but we're wetter."

"And I am sleek," said Mackerel,
"A swimmer that can shimmer."

"But people like you kill me,
And grill me up. I'm dinner!"

Nightjar

If you spot a bit of bark
That blinks at you, when all is dark,
That charms you with the song it sings,
That starts to flap and clap its wings,
Then that little bit of bark
Is not a bit of bark at all,
It's a little hidden nightjar
With a wicked little call.

Allis shad

Shimmer, glimmer, allis shad,
In your bright, silver coat.
Dash up river, allis shad,
Pretend you are a boat.

Swim up the Severn, allis shad,
Swim up the River Dart.
Drop off your eggs, allis shad,
And drift back to the start.

The Thrill Factor

ur	or

| thought | many | people | move | water |

The Thrill Factor is a non-fiction text in the form of a report.

Welcome, thrill-seekers! Read about three activities that will test your nerves to the limit! From the **colossus** Nemesis roller-coaster, famous for its **inverted** sections and sudden drops, to conquering your fear of fire. Find out how experts teach people to walk over hot coals and how the science behind **thermal conductors** makes this possible. Warning! Do not try this at home. This is an activity led by experts in controlled conditions.

And finally, discover the watery thrills of surfing. See how surfers **absorb** the immense force of waves to shred the curl!

Vocabulary:
- **colossus:** incredibly large
- **inverted:** upside down
- **thermal:** heat
- **conductors:** materials that can move heat or electricity easily
- **absorb:** to take on and reduce the intensity of something

Are you a thrill-seeker or not? Why do you think people like to be scared or do activities like these?

The Thrill Factor

If your guts churn at the thought of stepping off a kerb, or normal frights make you curl up, then this report is NOT for you.

But if you are a thrill-seeker, then we've got what you need!

Nemesis coaster

Thrill factor: Seven stars

Nemesis is a classic inverted coaster. It is in the form of a horned monster from a different planet, waiting to perform horrors on its victims.

Park visitors hang under the rails and attempt to withstand disturbing drops and organ-distorting turns. And all this at a gut-churning top speed of 81 km/h.

This absurd, curving colossus demands seven thrill factor stars.

Burning coals

Thrill factor: Three stars

Stepping on a thorn can hurt. But stepping on burning embers? The pain must be off the charts! This is so frightening that people are often sponsored to do it. You need proper support and training from experts to perform this skill.

It turns out that coals are bad thermal conductors. If you are quick and march on flat feet, you will not get burned.

Many people report feeling transformed after stepping across burning coals. They claim to feel confident and optimistic.

This transforming march calls for three thrill factor stars.

Surf school

Thrill factor: Six stars

If water sports are your thing, then the inland surf school in Bristol, UK, is perfect. You start on land to master important surfing skills, like paddling and popping up. Then you hurl yourself into the water and wait for a swell.

Surfers pop up and then coast along, attempting to absorb the shocks and keep standing up. Then they crash and burn onto the sand!

Better surfers can perform a move called 'shredding the curl' – a term to explain quick, curving turns that cut the water. Some perform a move called 'barrelling'.

This rip-curling sport gets six thrill factor stars.

Set an alarm for this time next week for part 2 of The Thrill Factor! Our absorbing report on zorbing will get you in a spin!

Challenge texts

The Alhambra

ai	ee

beautiful	house	through	English

The Alhambra is a travel blog written by a girl called Meena.

Meena's blog gives you a guided tour of the Alhambra in Spain. Find out about how this majestic **complex** of buildings and gardens was **constructed**. Discover the incredible Islamic craftmanship that created **turrets**, a **keep** (which is also a prison), as well as **tranquil** gardens, clever water systems and beautiful art. Read on to find out more about these ancient buildings set high in the hills of Granada, with **vistas** of the landscape below.

Vocabulary:
- **complex:** a group of buildings set in the same place
- **constructed:** made
- **turrets:** small towers on the corner of a wall
- **keep:** the strongest tower of a castle
- **tranquil:** quiet, calm and peaceful
- **vistas:** beautiful views

What place in the world do you have very strong feelings about?

The Alhambra

Meena's Must-Sees

Greetings from Spain! In today's blog, I visit the beautiful Alhambra in Granada. Come with me as I see all the riches of this majestic complex.

The Alhambra was constructed between 1238 and 1358. A Muslim king began to make this incredible house in 1238. Then two Muslim kings added to it to make the stunning complex we see today.

The Alhambra sits on a steep hill, with sweeping vistas beyond the treetops.

At the west of the Alhambra, you will see the Alcazaba. This dazzling spot has lots of turrets.

One of the turrets was a keep that held grain. It was a prison as well.

You can see the remains of Arab houses in the Alcazaba.

The Alhambra is a fantastic example of Islamic craftsmanship.

You will see Arabic script in the panels.

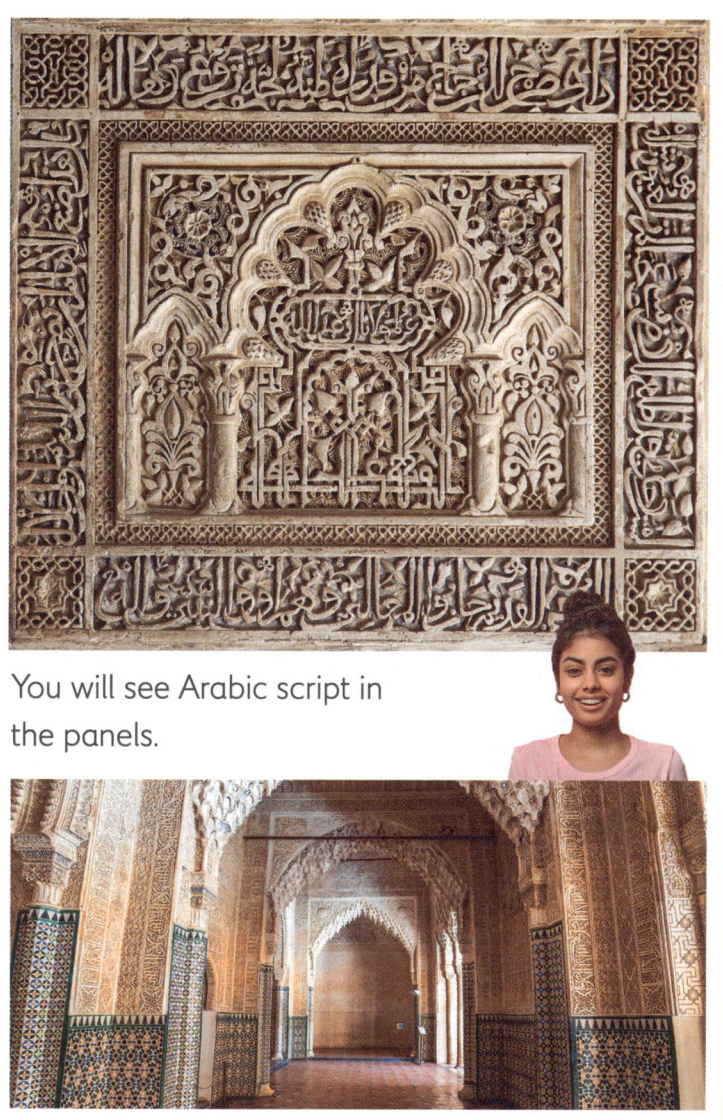

People do not just come to the Alhambra to see the craftsmanship. They come to see the plants as well. The vivid greens of the plants contrast with the restful water.

There is a deep forest of English elm trees at the Alhambra. Many people see this as a terrific spot to rest from the sun. I think you will agree!

Water runs all through the Alhambra. It trickles in lush, green spots where you can stop and relax. It runs in drains along the streets. It sits in tranquil ponds that reflect the Alhambra back at itself. It gushes out from between the teeth of big cats.

The Alhambra is top of my list when I visit Spain. It's difficult to explain the feeling as you go through it. There is so much to see, it is astonishing. I could visit again and again. I think you will love it.

Get your tickets quick, as they sell out!

The Lightning God

| igh | oa |

| anyone | who | their | house | many |

The Lightning God is a retelling of a Greek myth about the birth of Zeus. In Greek mythology, Zeus is a god and the King of Olympus. He is also known as the Lightning God.

This myth tells the story of how the Gods of Olympus were born and gained power. It starts with a terrible battle between the King of the Titans, Uranus, and his son Cronus. When Cronus wins the battle, Uranus makes an **oath** saying that Cronus will be crushed by his children! This **maddens** Cronus and, when he does have children of his own, he does something awful to make sure that they will not grow up and crush him.

But one tiny **infant** is hidden and survives to **blossom** into Zeus, a goatskin-**cloaked** god. Only one mystery remains: how will Zeus defeat Cronus and free his **siblings** ...?

Vocabulary:
- **oath:** a very serious promise
- **maddens:** makes someone extremely angry
- **infant:** a young child or baby
- **blossom:** to grow in a healthy way
- **cloaked:** wrapped up in a fabric or cloak
- **siblings:** brothers and sisters

How do you think Cronus stopped his children from growing up and crushing him?

The Lightning God

What a sight! See the might of the Lightning God, in his goatskin cloak.

He is so strong! He can chuck lightning bolts at anyone who maddens him.

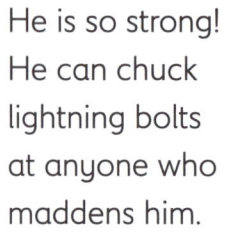

But when he was an infant, this god was at risk ... from his DAD! Let's go back in time ...

The Lightning God's dad was so bad that he attacked *his* dad, the King of the Gods. He *needed* to be king, you see. But as the King fell, croaking in pain, he made an oath.

"You cannot frighten me, Dad! I will not have kids. Simple!"

But this was impossible. The King of the Gods had to make the planet and to do that, he needed children to help him.

His queen was the bright Goddess of Beginnings and Endings, and she loved kids.

The Queen fell pregnant and, in time, their house was filled with the din of a screeching infant.

But in an instant, the selfish King ran to the Queen, grabbed the infant and chucked it into his gob!

This happened again and again, with many children.

The Queen was frightened of the King. But when she held their sixth kid, cloaked in a blanket, she made a high-risk plan.

She made an oath: "I will protect you."

She hid the infant with a trusted friend – a goat high up on the coast.

On that high hill, the goat fed the little god with goat milk. The infant blossomed into a strong adult. Then the goat gifted its skin to him, as a battle-cloak.

That strong adult developed into our Lightning God! It was time to fight his frightening dad.

The Lightning God freed his remaining siblings from his dad's rotten guts. He tricked his dad into gulping a disgusting drink. Then the King vomited up his children!

The Lightning God and his siblings crushed their dad. And so the Lightning God ended up as the King of the Gods.

Shark Attack

er	ar

their	people	waters	should	time

Shark Attack is an article that explores the relationship between people and sharks.

Sharks have a **sinister** reputation. But is that fair? This article argues that shark attacks are very rare. Sharks may be at the **pinnacle** of the food chain, but they feed on other **aquatic** mammals – not humans! It is only when sharks enter **coastal waters** where people are that these attacks occur.

Surfers can be mistaken for seals by sharks. Sometimes the shark **jerks** surfers under the water by the leg strap that attaches the surfer to their board. Read on to find out how the **residents** of **Perth** are protecting people and sharks.

Vocabulary:
- **sinister:** scary; threatening
- **pinnacle:** the highest point
- **aquatic:** growing or living in water
- **coastal waters:** the waters around the coast where people often swim
- **jerks:** tugs forcefully
- **residents:** the people who live in a place
- **Perth:** a large city in Western Australia

Do sharks deserve their sinister reputation? Why/why not?

SHARK ATTACK

Sharks are scattered across the planet, from the Greenland shark in the Arctic to the sleeper shark in Antarctica.

Greenland shark

Sharks are at the pinnacle of the feeding chain. They feed on starfish, squid and aquatic mammals – and on different sharks. But when sharks shift their sights to coasts where lots of people gather, then they can become a problem.

Sharks' sinister charcoal fins have become a common sight in the coastal waters of Perth, sparking alarm in residents.

But should people be frightened? Shark attacks in Perth are uncommon. There were just six attacks in 2024 and no one was killed by a shark in that time.

The SharkSmart app was developed in 2019. This sends swimmers alerts when sharks are sighted. But attacks do still happen.

In 2020, a teen called Sav was attacked by a 1.5 m shark. He said to start with, it felt like the shark was a weed brushing against his leg. Then, the shark jerked him under by his leg strap.

Sav stopped the attack by detaching the leg strap, and his friend paddled him to shelter. Sav had remarkable luck and was unharmed.

In March 2025, a man swimming off the Perth coast got bumped, battered and bitten by a shark. The swimmer yelled to attract a boat, and he scrambled in. The shark lingered. The man was seen by a GP, but didn't need to go to hospital.

What can Perth residents do to stop this pattern of attacks? The best method might be to keep sharks and swimmers apart. Shark experts have started to string shark nets across sheltered inlets that stop sharks from entering, so people are protected.

shark net

Shark nets and the SharkSmart app have helped the number of shark attacks to drop.

But sharks didn't attack people until we fished and swam in their habitats. So, if you consider sharks as monsters, think again. The fact is, people have encroached on their habitats.

Sharks don't expect people to be in the water. They could think people are otters, fish and sharks, so an attack might just be a blunder!

Perhaps people should just keep out of the water – what do you think?

Storm!

ur	or

worked	water	could	laughed

Storm! is an adventure story set at a holiday camp.

Kurt and Zaina are about to test out their raft, when the holiday camp dog, Dora, decides to join them. Despite the way that Dora makes the raft **lurch** in the water, the two friends are happy to have her along. But this test float is not going to be a simple trip ... A storm is **lurking** and soon the **relentless surf** is pounding the little raft. And as the raft reaches the **crests** of massive waves, Kurt and Zaina start to lose hope ...

Vocabulary:
- **lurch:** move suddenly in an uncontrolled way
- **lurking:** a hidden danger waiting just out of sight
- **relentless:** unstoppable
- **surf:** the waves as they break
- **crests:** the tops of waves

What do you think is the biggest danger for Kurt and Zaina right now?

Storm!

"Let's go!" said Kurt.

Zaina zipped up her jacket and slipped onto the raft. They had worked all morning at camp to get it afloat.

"Ha! Dora has turned up! That dog loves rafting," said Zaina.

Dora burst onto the bank and the raft lurched as she jumped on.

Kurt grinned. "I'm glad we didn't sink! Let's go for a short float and test this raft out."

Dora wagged at the water.

"Any mermaids lurking in the surf?" asked Kurt.

"Ha-ha. Our raft is intact! I'm glad we factored in some extra floats. It feels just right," said Zaina.

"I agree," said Kurt.

"Let's float to the north. Then we can turn back," said Zaina.

But as they turned to the north, Zaina spotted a black mist forming …

A sudden gust of wind made the raft lurch and toss in the churning surf.

"I think the raft might get torn apart!" exclaimed Kurt.

"It's important that we turn back!" yelled Zaina.

The wind was getting stronger, and they struggled to make the raft turn in the relentless surf.

Then a flash of lightning forked up high. The wind pushed and the raft was tugged out, speeding far from camp.

"The storm is so strong that I cannot get the raft to turn!" said Zaina.

Just then, Dora sprang into the water.

"Dora!" yelled Kurt in alarm.

Zaina could just see a flash of the dog's fur in the churning water. But then Dora started to tug the raft!

Dora surfed on the crests. She dragged the raft, pulling it hard.

"It's turning!" said Kurt.

Dora turned the raft into the wind. Paddling hard, Zaina and Kurt pushed with all their might. They cut into the churning water, straining their arms to fight the wind.

"We cannot let the storm win!" insisted Zaina.

In time, they made it back onto the sand.

"It turns out *Dora* is a mermaid!" laughed Kurt.

Dora flicked water from her wet fur onto Kurt and Zaina.

"It's raining dog!" giggled Zaina.

"Come and get some lunch! It's burgers and chips today," called the camp mentor.

Dora barked.

"Yes, we will get some lunch for our mermaid dog as well!" said Kurt, patting Dora.

"Perhaps a hot dog?" grinned Zaina.

Consolidate texts

Travel to TRAPPIST-1e

ai	ee

| your | want | don't | like | friends | time |

Travel to TRAPPIST-1e is a travel guide made to persuade people to choose it as their holiday destination.

Imagine a time when we can travel to distant planets and can see the sun set in another world! TRAPPIST-1e is a **hot spot** for space travellers who want some adventure but also want to relax and eat great food. Travel on a **shuttle** to your **hostel** where treetop **trails** await you. What strange creatures will you discover in the Sweet **Mist Plains**? Are you brave enough to try the green **shrimp** hot dogs? Don't wait, dive into your next planetary adventure!

Vocabulary:
- **hot spot:** a popular place
- **shuttle:** a bus that goes back and forth between two places
- **hostel:** a relaxed, cheap place to stay
- **trails:** paths
- **mist:** like a cloud that is close to the ground
- **plains:** large, flat areas of land with very few trees
- **shrimp:** a small sea creature that's like a prawn

Do you think that humans will ever be able to go on holiday to other planets? What do you think we will find?

Travel to TRAPPIST-1e

Visit TRAPPIST-1e!

This spring, visit TRAPPIST-1e! Treetop trails and chatting chimpanzees await you on the pinkest planet of all!

Let your brain relax and rock-et to sleep on the three-week trip to the planet.

No need to wait, your shuttle will speed you to your rock-top hostel. Then relax with a green mocktail and see the endless sunset. You will see planets as well!

Trip 1: Black treetop trail

Do you want to chat with TRAPPIST chimpanzees? Then don't wait! Get on the black treetop trail and meet them.

Trip 2: Sweet-smelling mists

What is that smell? It's the toffee mist that sweeps across the Sweet Mist Plains.

This is where you can see painted snails feed on wobble weed.

Trip 3: Lunch like a queen!

The TRAPPIST Queen is a lunchtime hot spot! Meet with friends to sip rain-tree coffee and nibble green shrimp hot dogs.

Trip 4: Gift shopping

Finish your trip with sweet gifts from Toffee Mists gift shop. Then travel back to the hostel and have a long sleep!

Lightwing

| igh | oa |

| today | friend | yourself | through |

Lightwing is a graphic novel set in the mythical world of Ancient Egypt.

When Tad finds a treasure map, he convinces his friend Lightwing, a phoenix, to come with him to find **riches** beyond their wildest dreams! But this is not going to be an **uneventful** trip. One minute, Tad and Lightwing are **coasting along** high above the land, when a griffin has a **disagreement** with them. Will Tad be able to find the treasure and **gloat** over his **swag**? Will the god, **Amun**, give Lightwing the speed and skill she needs?

Vocabulary:
- **riches:** treasure and gold
- **uneventful:** without any drama or bad things happening
- **coasting along:** moving with no effort
- **disagreement:** a fight or argument
- **gloat:** feel very clever about doing something
- **swag:** goods; valuables; treasures
- **Amun:** the Egyptian god of the air

What other challenges might Tad and Lightwing face?

Lightwing

"This slight disagreement with a griffin was not in my plan!"

Like a flash of lightning, Lightwing went sweeping out of the griffin's talons.

"Frightened? Me? I don't think so!"

Lightwing floated through a rock to get free of the griffin.

Thank Amun!

But this was not the right time to relax ...

I clung onto Lightwing's throat in shock.

You did it again, Lightwing!

Blinking with astonishment, I loaded my bag with swag.

You can have a present, Lightwing!

The bright rings twinkled on Lightwing's sleek neck. And on the uneventful trip back, I relaxed at last!

Killer Instinct

er	ar

by	their	people	water	where

Killer Instinct is a non-fiction text.

Which animal has the best chance of hunting, catching and then eating their dinner? Well, the answers might surprise you! All the animals here have the **stamina**, speed and cleverness to **target** and **track** their prey and **adapt** their plans if needed. Some, like the mantis, **linger** in the grass that they **resemble**, before making a sudden attack. Others, like African painted dogs, work as a team to run down their **victim**. All these animals are expert killers, but which is the most successful?

Vocabulary:
- **stamina:** ability to keep on going over a long distance or time
- **target:** choose (e.g. an animal to hunt)
- **track:** follow
- **adapt:** change
- **linger:** wait for a long time
- **resemble:** look like something else
- **victim:** an animal that is hurt or killed

Which animal do you think is the most successful at catching its dinner?

KILLER INSTINCT

Some animals are expert hunters. They never want to miss a kill – ever! They adapt to habitats and hunt by sight and smell with skill, speed and stamina.

But what animals target and track their dinner the best?

Mantis

The mantis is harmless to people, but it is an expert killer of grasshoppers. It blends into its habitat and lingers, resembling grass. It remains sharp and alert as it keeps out of sight.

Then it starts a sudden attack! It springs out, grabs its target with lightning speed and grasps its dinner with its strong legs.

Archer fish

Rather than hunting in the water, the archer fish prefers insects. It floats by the top of the river until it spots its target. Then it spits out an arch of water! This blasts the insect off its branch and under the water, where the fish can munch it.

If it misses, the archer fish can jump high out of the water to grab its dinner!

African painted dog

African painted dogs are stronger in numbers than apart. They hunt in packs of 6 to 25, to get bigger kills. They single out their victim and track it until it comes to a standstill. Then they fight with their sharp teeth and gulp their dinner as quick as they can.

African painted dogs kill 80% of their targets, marking them as one of Africa's best hunters.

Dragon Quest

| ur | or |

| friends | people | thought | minutes |

Dragon Quest is a fantasy adventure story.

The people of Hurn are being attacked by monsters **thronging** around their coast. The Lords get together and decide to send a young warrior, Ved, on a quest to persuade the dragon king to join forces with them. Ved will have many challenges, but the biggest **hurdle** of all will be repairing trust between the dragons and the people of Hurn. In the **midst** of an epic battle with a **basilisk**, help comes for Ved from the skies. But will Ved's rescuer **regret** saving a human?

Vocabulary:
- **thronging:** great numbers of animals or humans moving around in a place
- **hurdle:** a challenge
- **midst:** the middle of
- **basilisk:** a mythical reptile, often shown with the head of a cockerel
- **regret:** to feel sad or disappointed about something that you have done

Who do you think has helped Ved?

Dragon Quest

The Lords of Hurn sent Ved on a quest. "Return with the dragon king. It must defend us from the monsters that lurk off the north coast," they said.

The road to the dragon's den was full of hazards. The biggest hurdle was the Basilisk.

As Ved passed a bent thorn tree, the Basilisk burst out. It rushed to fight Ved with talons like steel. But then a scorching blast burned the Basilisk's tail, and it fled.

Ved gasped as the dragon king swept out of the darkness in a storm of purple wings.

Ved turned to the dragon king. In dragon speech, he said, "The Lords ask you to defend Hurn from the monsters."

A spurt of sparks burst from the dragon king's lips. "The Lords killed my friends. But still they ask for my help?" it snarled.

Ved nodded. "If you return, you will profit from it. The Lords will end their battle with the dragons. The people of Hurn and the dragons will be as one again."

The dragon thought hard. "I'll go," it said.

Ved jumped on the dragon's back. In a short time, they were at the coast. The port was thronging with monsters, but the dragon king stormed into their midst. With one burning blast, it shrivelled their commander. In minutes, the last of the monsters had fled.

The Lords turned to the dragon.

They said, "We regret what we did to your friends. Thank you for defending us. In return for your support, we will make you King of Hurn."

And from then on, dragons and people were as one.